SUPERCELL - A NOVELLA

CRITICAL INCIDENT #1

DOUGLAS DOROW

SuperCell

Critical Incident #1

A novella
by Douglas Dorow

ABOUT SUPERCELL - CRITICAL INCIDENT #1

The FBI's Hostage Rescue team is called to the plains of Nebraska when a supercell storm sweeps across the state and hits the Nebraska State Penitentiary, a maximum security prison.

Chaos strikes the prison and two inmates escape.

Special Agent Ross Fruen is on his first assignment with the HRT after transferring into the team.

SuperCell is a spin-off novella from The Ninth District - FBI thriller #1.

For updates on new releases, exclusive promotions and other information, sign up for Douglas Dorow's Thriller Reader list

R oss Fruen walked through the dormitory looking for his room. His footsteps echoed down the hall. He had a pack across his back and a duffel bag grasped in his right hand. The air-conditioning was helping, but it couldn't quite match the heat and humidity of the afternoon. Sweat dribbled down his back between his shoulder blades and formed on his forehead.

He'd forgotten about the constant popping noise from the gun range. Or had just grown so used to it when he was here before that he didn't notice it.

Quantico hadn't changed much since he completed his training as an FBI special agent.

His assignment papers said he was sharing a room with two agents; Stevens and Rupert. He squeezed past a couple of agents in training wearing matching blue t-shirts. "Room 115?" he asked.

"Keep going. Down on your left, Sir," one of them answered.

Sir? Some things didn't change; the new agents in

training always helpful, always polite, thinking they're always being evaluated.

Ross found the room and stood outside the open door. So, these were the quarters for the FBI's Hostage Rescue Team. He took a deep breath. OK, ready. He stepped into the room. There were two beds, one on either side, just like he remembered, built in desks, dressers and closets, linoleum tiled floor, an overhead fluorescent light.

An oscillating fan slowly turned back and forth blowing air across the room. Yep, things hadn't changed much. On the bed to his right, there was a guy lying on his back, napping. On the bed to his left, there was a dog curled up, napping. Now, *that's* different, he thought. There weren't dogs in the rooms before. The dog's ear twitched and he opened one eye to look at Ross.

Ross cleared his throat and set his bags down on the floor. The guy opened his eyes. "Hey," Ross said. "My papers say I'm assigned here, with agents Stevens and Rupert."

The man swung his legs out of bed. Feet on the floor, he yawned and rubbed the sleep from his eyes. He looked Ross over and stood. He wore shorts and a white tank top. He was about Ross' height, six foot one inch, maybe a little taller, and broader in the shoulders. One shoulder bore a tattoo, his dark hair was cut short, his head was tanned. He crossed the room and stuck out his hand. "I'm Stevens." He pointed at the dog. "And this is Rupert."

Ross shook hands and looked Stevens in the eye. He had a firm grip, dark eyes, and a mixture of seriousness and fun in his stare.

"Ross Fruen. Wasn't expecting one of my roommates was

a dog." Rupert hopped off the bed and walked over to sniff Ross' pants.

"Go ahead, kneel down and get to know him, you're part of the team, part of the pack where the dogs are concerned," urged Stevens.

Ross hung his arm down and let Rupert sniff the back of his hand. "I'm not real good with dogs."

"Rupert will change your mind, once you get to know him." Stevens reached down and grabbed one of Ross' bags and placed the bag on the bed. "Now he knows that's your bed. He'll leave it alone now." Stevens lay back down on his own bed and flicked his hand. Rupert found his dog bed at the foot of Stevens' and curled into a ball to nap again.

"He reads your mind?" Ross asked.

Stevens smiled. "Sometimes it seems like it. We've been partners for a long time."

Ross started emptying his bags onto his bed, sorting items into the appropriate piles before he placed them in the right drawer or shelf in the closet and dresser next to his bed. "I didn't know HRT had dogs."

"They didn't. We're the first handler, dog team."

"Not FBI?" Ross asked.

"We weren't. We are now. I was Army, finishing up my duty in Afghanistan working with Rupert. We had a couple of HRT guys in our unit looking for terrorists. Somebody in the FBI asked what I was going to do next and talked me into joining the FBI after they negotiated with the military to let Rupert come with me. We're an experiment. Just finished our training and got our initial assignment. What's your story?"

Ross moved a couple of things to make room and sat on his bed. "Another new guy, another experiment. I'm an agent, but they let me into HRT before I completed the mandatory two years as a field agent. I was in Minneapolis on my first assignment after graduating from the academy. Helped solve a big case and they gave me my choice of next assignments. I heard HRT was staffing up, so I asked to be placed here. Just got assigned to Palmer's team here after completing my HRT training."

"Well, welcome to the team." Stevens stood and grabbed a tennis ball. Rupert stood at attention. "Time for us to go play. We'll leave you to get settled. Our team's up tonight in the shoot house at nineteen hundred hours. See you there."

THE PLAINS OF NEBRASKA

The lights flickered and the cell block went dark. The emergency siren repeated its warning, blaring again and again. Back-up lights illuminated the halls and the exits casting shadows along the walls. Inmates yelled, whistled, screamed and laughed. Joe Kelly stood at the door of his cell, palms placed against the solid metal door, head cocked to one side, listening, taking it all in.

"What's going on, Joe?" Tommy Martinelli yelled from across the hall. Tommy was new to the maximum security prison sitting on the plains of Nebraska, a wind-break pelted by sand in the summer and snow in the winter as winds blew from Colorado to Iowa. He'd played junior college football, defensive tackle, where his size and temper made him lethal. He was also lethal off the field and that's why he was here. He killed an old farmer and his wife when they caught him trying to steal some of their cattle to support his drug habit.

"Just a storm, Tommy!" Joe yelled back. "Nothing to worry about. The Corn Crib isn't going anywhere." Joe Kelly had called the Nebraska State Penitentiary - maximum security prison, commonly referred to as The Crib, home for five years. It was his second prison home. He had been in a prison in Missouri serving his second year of a twenty-year sentence for a murder during a jewelry store robbery, when he was transferred here. He was transferred after he killed a fellow inmate and critically injured a prison guard. In his five years in The Crib, he'd seen everything Mother Nature had to throw at the place.

"I feel trapped, Joe! I want to be able to see outside!"

Joe yelled back during the silence between the blaring alarm signal. "Just sit down...and relax. ... They'll turn the horns off...soon enough."

Hugh Hancock stood in front of the green screen in his white shirt, sleeves rolled up to his elbows, his tie hanging loosely around his neck. He shifted from foot to foot and bounced on the balls of his feet. Meteorologists lived for this moment. The camera light turned on signaling he was live.

"At four-thirty this afternoon, the National Weather Service issued a tornado warning for Baxter and Henry Counties in central Nebraska. Everyone in the path of this storm should seek immediate shelter." Off camera, he watched the monitor to see the picture of the weather front behind him. The clicker to toggle the image was in the palm of his right hand. Stepping to the side, he swept his arms to show how the two storm cells were merging.

"Doppler radar indicates we have two massive supercells meeting southwest of Thompson. There are reports of multiple funnel clouds, so please seek shelter at this time.

Get to your basements and cellars and tune into us on your radios for continued weather updates."

He shifted to the other side, turned to look at the screen and changed the image. "There are reports of hail along the leading edge of this storm. Temperatures are dropping rapidly." He put his hand up to his ear to better hear through his earpiece. "We have a report of a funnel on the ground near the intersection of County Roads I and Twenty-One and it's moving to the northeast towards Thompson. I repeat, if you are in the path of this storm, anywhere near Thompson you should seek immediate shelter."

FBI ACADEMY - QUANTICO, VIRGINIA

"New guy, Agent Fruen, you're up."

Ross tensed after the team leader called his name. His gut twinged like he'd made the plunge on an amusement park roller coaster and the temperature in the room felt like it jumped twenty degrees. He wiped the sweat from his forehead and moved to the front of the group. Time to prove he was ready. His job to lead them on their first run of the night through the maze of rubber-coated walls of the shooting house, configured to represent the floor plan of a house. As the first one through the doors, he was the eyes for those behind him. He was also the one most at risk of getting shot if they encountered any bad guys along the way.

Even though this was only a drill, everything seemed real. Dressed for combat, weapons loaded with live ammo, the team took up positions behind him. They were like a football team lined up at the line of scrimmage waiting for the snap of the ball to unleash their power. A soundtrack played over speakers with the creaks and groans of a building and the sounds of traffic and barking dogs outside a house. Concentration zoomed into the task at hand. Ross started forward deliberately, heel-toe across the floor to the closed door, his MP5 pointed ahead of him, ready to shoot any unfriendlies in his path. The team moved behind him as one.

At the door, he stepped to the side and the agent behind him applied a strip of explosive charges around the side edges of the door by the hinges and the door knob. Everyone turned away from the door and the agent counted down with his fingers, three, two, one. A small explosion and Ross immediately turned and pushed the door into the room, where it fell flat to the floor. He followed it in and swept his eyes and his gun to the right, assessing the room in a blink of an eye. An enemy target stood in the corner. He shot it with two quick shots, center mass. An agent was right behind him, covering the room to the left, a third took the center. He knew they were there without looking because that's where they were supposed to be. They quickly regrouped to move on to the next room. There was no time to assess or evaluate. They needed to keep moving.

An open doorway in the far, left corner appeared to lead down a hallway. Ross peeked around the corner. The hallway was clear. He signaled and led the way, again in a slight crouch, light footsteps, his entire focus ahead of him. He knew his teammates were behind him checking the rear and one over each shoulder maximizing the firepower and vision ahead of them while making as small of a target as possible.

Ten feet ahead another hallway ran perpendicular to the one they were in. When they reached the corner, the agent on the left used his left hand to toss a flashbang grenade around the corner and down the next hallway. The bang and concussion was the signal to proceed. Anyone in the hallway would be temporarily stunned.

Ross moved to enter the hallway. Someone grabbed the neck of his protective vest, yanked him back and pushed him into the wall.

"What're you doing?"

Ross stayed silent, sensing it wasn't a question he was supposed to answer.

"Look, then enter. Just 'cuz we flashbanged the hall doesn't mean they can't shoot. They might just start firing blindly down the hall and catch you with a bullet as you round the corner." The patch over the agent's heart read "Palmer". "You did OK, up to here, for an effin' new guy. But always look before you leap. We can't afford to carry you out and I don't want the extra paperwork. "

Palmer, the lead, watched Ross, evaluating him, coaching him. They didn't know each other yet and this was Ross' first drill with the team. Ross knew he had to prove himself to Palmer and the rest of the team. He nodded and moved to get to the "ready" position back at the corner to the hallway.

Palmer stood behind him and tapped him on the shoulder. "OK, Agent Fruen, let's try it again. This time let's send the dog down the hallway first."

Ross glanced behind him and found Stevens. His partner, Rupert, part shepherd, part lab and part Cujo crazy, stood alert at his side, dressed for battle in a ballistic vest and head gear. Ross signaled them up. Rupert was ready to go, in a slight squat, his haunches like springs ready for action. "We need to send in the dog and see what's up ahead around that corner," Ross explained to Stevens.

"We've got it, roomie." Stevens checked the video output from the camera strapped to Rupert's head to make sure they'd have a visual. He sent the dog on his way with a few hand signals and a command, "Rupert, Vooruit."

Ross glanced at Stevens and then Rupert, not sure what Stevens had said.

Rupert crept down the hallway, hugging the wall until he got to the corner. Ross covered him with his weapon. Stevens monitored the video feed, whispered updates into his microphone and Rupert heard his commands in the small speaker stuck into his ear.

NEBRASKA

"Tornado sighting, tornado sighting, this is not a drill!" The warning sounded over the loudspeakers and echoed down the prison hallways. Joe Kelly forced a yawn to equalize the pressure in his ears. The weather front moving past outside must be severe if he could feel the pressure change like this. He moved to the corner of his cell and squatted, preparing for the worst.

"Jooooooe!" Tommy yelled from across the hall.

Kelly stayed in his spot against the wall. The Crib was heavily fortified, but that didn't mean he'd be foolish and stand at the door. Better to be safe, than sorry. Back against the wall. Heels pulled into his butt. He cleared his ears again, bent his head and put his face into his thighs and covered the back of his head with his hands. Around him it sounded like a freight train was approaching and passing on the other side of the wall. He felt the wall vibrating against his back, like the building itself was afraid of the oncoming storm. He closed his eyes and took a deep breath.

~

AN EXPLOSION ROCKED THE CRIB. Kelly held his tucked position and felt sand and dust raining down on the backs of his hands. Then he felt something wet hit. He put his hand in front of his face and looked at it. Something liquid hit his head. He looked up and saw a three-foot gash in the ceiling. Rain was coming through the hole into his cell.

"Jooooe! You OK?" Tommy yelled from across the hall.

Kelly stood and looked up at the hole while he walked to the door. "Tommy, there's a hole in the roof in here. You OK?"

"Yeah, what the hell happened?" Tommy yelled back.

"I think that tornado made a direct hit on us." Joe looked back up at the hole. "Is your cell OK?"

"Mine's good!"

Kelly heard a lot of yelling out in the hallway. "Hey, Tommy, hang on! Sounds like something's going on out there!" Then he heard the familiar sound of the automatic cell doors unlocking. Next, as if by magic, his door slid open and he watched across the hall as Tommy's opened too.

Tommy stepped into the hallway, looked one way, then the other. "Come on, Joe, let's go." He stood in the hallway, holding his arms out, enjoying the freedom.

Joe took a step into the hallway. Sirens started blaring. Not the weather sirens, but the prison's emergency sirens they heard when officers were needed to respond to some sort of prisoner conflict. A shotgun blast echoed from the walls down to his left. Followed by another. He grabbed Tommy's shirt and tugged him back into his own cell.

"What're you doing? This may be our chance to get out of here."

"Or get shot, trying," Joe answered. Then the cell door automatically started to slide shut.

Tommy jumped to the door and tried to slow its closure.

He grabbed the edge of the door, but it didn't slow and continued closing until it was sealed and locked. He turned and looked at Kelly. "Now we're fucked."

HUGH HANCOCK LOOKED into the camera. "We have witnesses who are reporting a tornado has touched down and damaged the Nebraska maximum security prison. No reports of injuries at this time, but we are waiting to hear. Word is that the prison is secure."

JOE LOOKED up at the hole in the ceiling. He couldn't reach it alone, it was too high. But together they might be able to reach it. "You ready to get out of here?" he asked. "If we're going to do it, we have to do it now while everything is still crazy."

"Let's do it. We'll never get another chance like this," Tommy answered.

Joe grabbed the blanket from his bed and stood in the corner below the hole. "Give me a boost up. Once I'm through I'll tie off the blanket up there and you can use it to climb up while I pull you up."

"GOOD THING I'm in the cell across the hall from you and not Chip." Tommy said. "That tub of lard would've never squeezed his fat ass through that hole."

"Well, you almost didn't make it through. For a minute there, I thought I was going to have to leave you behind.

That's why I stay lean and mean. You're never too skinny to fit through something," Joe said.

They were on the roof of the prison. It looked like a bomb had exploded. The tornado had carried a lot of debris with it and when it hit the prison some of the debris, including cars and trucks, had slammed into the wall. Joe didn't understand the science of it, but something had opened up a crack where his ceiling met the walls. On the roof of the prison, huge air-conditioning units were torn from their mounts and lay in a heap along with car bodies, wood, trees and other garbage.

"Must've been one hell of a tornado," Joe said.

"Never thought I'd say this, but I'm glad we were inside," Tommy said.

They cautiously walked to the edge of the building, stepping over the debris while they looked around to make sure nobody saw them. It was dark out and lights still lit up the ground below, except where they had been torn out by the storm. Joe pointed to the strip of dark ground. "That's our only chance. Going out while it's still dark, through there. They'll all be focused on the inside with all of the mayhem going on."

"Then, what?" Tommy asked.

"One step at a time. It's not like we have a plan. We'll need to improvise while we go. But we have to go now, or not at all."

They ripped the blanket into four strips, tied the pieces together and secured one end to the carcass of a rooftop air-conditioning unit and dropped the other end over the side of the building. "I'll go first," Joe said. "I'm going to hit the ground and walk straight out into the dark. I'll go a ways out and wait for you. Don't run. We'll attract less attention just walking. Give me about a ten second head start. That way you'll know if I'm seen or not."

Tommy stuck out his hand. "Good luck." They shook hands. "I'll be right behind you."

Joe slipped over the side and held onto the blanket, kind of sliding and lowering himself hand over hand towards the ground. Three sections of the makeshift rope hung over the side of the building leaving a five or six foot drop to the ground. As he reached the last section and all of his weight was supported by it, he felt it start to move. The knot was slipping. He let go, not quite sure how far he had to fall. He bent his knees to absorb the impact, hit the ground, let his legs collapse and rolled onto his back, then over onto his stomach. A quick check of his arms and legs, everything seemed OK. He quickly looked around. He didn't see anyone, so he pushed himself up to his feet and walked away from the prison into the dark.

When he reached the count of eight he looked back to see how Tommy was doing. He saw that the makeshift rope was going to stand out against the side of the building. He wished they had thought of a way to remove it so it wasn't visible for the guards to see how they'd escaped right away. Tommy started down from the roof. Joe watched as Tommy lowered himself towards the ground. "Come on, Tommy," he whispered. When he reached the last section of the blanket Joe reflexively crossed his fingers, hoping the knot would hold until Tommy got to the end and had a shorter distance to drop. "Shit," he said, when he saw the knot slip and Tommy fall to the ground.

Tommy let out a muffled scream when he hit the ground. His legs hit cockeyed and one buckled. Joe crouched and waited to see if he was OK or if anyone heard him. He prepared to run if he had to.

TOMMY ROLLED onto his stomach and pushed himself up onto one leg, the good one. He tried walking towards Joe, but he was limping heavily. He stopped and looked out into the dark. Joe considered leaving him, but he didn't want to leave any sign of his escape behind. The blanket that was hanging down the wall from the roof had rebounded back onto the roof when the knot slipped, the tension slinging it up and the wind helping to push it back onto the roof. On the ground, by the wall was the bottom section of the blanket and Tommy. Joe eased up and quickly walked back to the wall. He grabbed the blanket off the ground and walked back to Tommy. "Put your arm over my shoulder, let's go."

"Thanks for coming back for me, Joe. Think I sprained my fucking ankle."

"Yeah. Let's get out of here and find a place to stop and check out your leg."

JOE AND TOMMY walked away from the prison quickly, like a couple of kids in a three-legged race. Tommy limped every other step while Joe supported him. Ahead of them about two hundred yards, a red, Ford pick-up truck stood in the road. "Hey, look what somebody left for us," Joe said.

The cab was a little crushed, looking like it had rolled across the road a few times. "Think it's driveable?" Tommy asked.

"Shh, listen." They stopped walking. "Sounds like it's still running. Let's go." Joe led them up to the truck. "Still has all four wheels. Anything is better than walking, especially with your ankle the way it is."

A man hung out of the open driver's door. The cab over the driver's seat was pushed about halfway down. Over the passenger seat, the cab was even with the bed of the pickup. "Is he dead?" Tommy asked.

Joe nudged the man and then pulled him out of the truck. "He must've been trying to ride out the storm in the truck. The truck's in Park. Whoever he is, he doesn't need a truck now." Joe checked the man's pockets and pulled out a wallet and a mobile phone. He looked at Tommy and then inside the cab. "We can't both fit in there. Let's get you in back. You can lay in the bed. I'll drive."

"Should we leave him or take him with us?"

Joe thought for a moment and then answered, "Let's throw him in back. We can get rid of him later." He dragged the body over to the side of the truck, lifted it up and dumped it in the back.

Tommy limped over to the truck and lifted his bad leg off the ground as he gripped the edge of the bed. "Give me a hand and let's get out of here."

Joe helped push Tommy into the bed of the pickup and then climbed behind the wheel. He bent over so he could see out between the roof of the cab and the dash. Then he applied the brake and shifted into Drive. A couple of test turns of the steering wheel and he was ready to go.

"Where are we going, anyway?" Tommy asked.

"How's your Spanish?"

"Dos cervezas por favor."

Joe laughed. "You're ready. We're heading to Mexico, mi amigo" He stepped on the gas and they were on their way.

"THOSE OF YOU IN BAXTER, if you're in your basements, you'll be staying a while longer. If you aren't, you should get there quickly, if you can." Hugh looked into the camera in all seriousness. "The second wave is coming, so sit tight."

The picture behind him changed. "For those who can see me, this picture behind me tells the story. But let me describe it in detail for those who can only hear me. "There's a large hook echo to the northeast and a second front is marching along the same path as the first. This second front may spout some additional tornadic activity."

FBI ACADEMY - QUANTICO, VIRGINIA

"That was a good session. You two are pretty amazing to watch together." Ross sat on his bed, tired physically and mentally.

"We're fitting in and Rupert's getting used to the drill and the team." Stevens scratched Rupert behind the ears and under his neck. "We're more used to operating outside, not so much close quarters indoors work. You did a good job of leading."

"I don't know," Ross answered. "I made a mistake and Palmer was all over me."

"That's his job. Don't sweat it."

Ross shook his head. "I can't afford to make mistakes. I'm here without the mandatory years of experience. I feel they're just looking for me to make a mistake."

"Snap out of it. They need you." Stevens grabbed Rupert's neck and scratched him behind the ears. "They need us. They're down on numbers so they're relaxing the requirements. You're in. Rupert and I are in. Just do the job and you'll be fine." Stevens laid back on his bed. "Think they'll let us sleep in after a night session?"

"I doubt it, so I'm going to see if I can get to sleep. Hopefully the adrenaline wears off and I crash hard."

"Sleep tight," Stevens said and then he signaled Rupert that it was downtime and the dog found his spot at the foot of the bed and curled up to rest. "I think we all need it."

Ross stared at the ceiling in the dark. "Let me ask you something."

"What?"

"When you sent Rupert down the hallway, you gave him some weird sounding verbal command."

Stevens answered in the dark. "All of his commands are in Dutch. That's how he was trained. It's how a lot of the military and police dogs are trained. There are some Czech, some Dutch. I had to learn the commands and how to say them close enough that he'd respond."

"So he wouldn't listen to me?"

"Not in English for sure, and probably not if you tried the Dutch commands. At least, not now. Maybe if we trained him together after a while he might." Stevens paused. "And it helps when the bad guys are trying to give him commands. Whether it's in English or Dutch, he ignores them."

"Good to know," Ross replied. "Is the dog going to snore tonight?"

Stevens laughed. "He was asking me the same thing about you."

LIGHTS FLASHED and an alarm repeated its signal. Ross pulled himself out of the dream he was having.

Rupert barked.

Over the intercom Ross heard "*Silver team deploy to the*

gymnasium. Silver team deploy to the gymnasium. This is not a drill."

"Is this a dream?" he asked Stevens. The clock showed they'd been asleep for a couple of hours.

"More like a nightmare."

They quickly got dressed. Ross knew that while they were getting ready there were other support members of HRT moving pre-packed cargo containers into trucks, planes or helicopters, depending on where they were going. They'd have everything needed when they got there, wherever there was. They'd find out soon enough. Ross and Stevens grabbed their GO bags. They were always packed and ready so they could deploy at a moment's notice.

"Let's go do some good," Ross said, and the three of them headed towards the gym.

EVERYONE RALLIED IN THE GYM. Looking around the group Ross could see that some of the team looked as groggy as he felt, while others looked rested and ready to go. There was a tension in the air and nervous joking. No one was talking about where they were going.

They were a core team of eleven, with Rupert a dozen. Stevens, Rupert and Ross were A Teamers, along with Ramirez. First ones through the doors. There were two snipers and floaters who either partnered with the snipers, taking notes, served as tacticians and logistics and communications for the team or joined the bangers. The other three were bangers and rappellers. They knocked down doors, overwhelmed, and restrained and contained as the team stormed through a location. The twelfth was Palmer - Control. The team's brain and decision maker once they got on location. He was on-site to talk with local police, coordinate resources and be the touch point back with the leaders at Quantico.

Palmer strode into the room and all talking ceased. "Gentlemen, we've got a mission. A tornado has touched down on the ground in Nebraska and damaged the maximum security prison there. Inmates have control of parts of the prison and have taken some of the guards hostage. They may get it under control, but we're heading out in case they don't. Briefing packets will be passed out en route. Any questions?" Palmer looked around the room, his stare drilling into each member of the team, one by one. He nodded and gave the order. "Saddle up."

THERE WAS a squadron of Blackhawks with pilots on standby at Quantico ready to ferry HRT teams around the globe to hotspots on a moment's notice. Just like everything else they drilled for, they'd drilled how to load into the Hawk. They didn't have time to waste. They'd loaded their gear and taken assigned seats in a matter of minutes. Ross got in last, the new member of the team. Johnson pointed to a seat and buckled in. The Blackhawk helicopter lifted into the air, hovered for a second, and they were on their way heading west running away from the sun. Briefing packets were passed out with instructions to digest and be ready in twenty minutes to talk through strategies and backup plans. The Omaha field office was closest to the scene and would have people on the ground providing updates while they were en-route.

Ross flipped through the briefing packet; eight hours with fuel stops. ETA 11:45 local time. They'd be there before lunch. There were overhead photos of the prison and layout drawings and schematics along with information on the prison population, the number of prisoners and guards on shift when the storm hit. When they landed they'd be up against a group of some of the most violent criminals in a contained environment that they knew well. The weather forecast was included too. The storm that had spawned the tornado had passed, but another was on its heels.

NEBRASKA

Tommy pounded on the crushed roof of the pickup. "Joe, we need to find someplace to hunker down."

Joe took his foot off the accelerator and the pickup slowed, shaking as it coasted to a stop. "What's up?" Joe yelled back through the broken window.

"See those clouds up ahead? The only time I've seen those is when a bad storm is coming. See the clouds? Puke green, all mixed up. That's not good."

"We already had a tornado."

"We could have another. If we're out here and it starts to hail, then you know you're fucked."

A couple of pea sized balls of ice bounced off the hood of the pickup "Hang on. There's a farmhouse about a half-mile up the road ahead of us." Joe gave the truck some gas.

THE PICKUP SKIDDED to a stop in the gravel drive of the farm. Hail pounded a drum solo on the truck. The farm yard was strewn with boards and tree limbs. A red barn lay in front of them. Its walls gone, the roof resting on the ground looking like the barn had lain down and gone to sleep. A brick silo stood sentry over them. Where the farm house stood was an old stone foundation covered with the remnants of what used to be there. Joe spied red storm cellar doors on the far side of the foundation. He weaved the truck through the yard to reach it.

Tommy swung down out of the pickup bed and stood next to the driver's window. "Let's go. I'm getting beat up here." He hopped over to the door on his good leg.

Joe climbed out the truck and put his arms over his head to protect it from the hail. At the storm cellar he pulled the door open. Its hinges squealed. A white light glowed from the cellar. Holding the door open, he helped Tommy as he stepped over a ledge onto the stone steps that led down. "Careful," he whispered. "Somebody's down there."

"HELLO?" Joe yelled down into the cellar. Tommy limped down the steps ahead of him. Joe lowered the steel doors and the drumming drowned out any sounds below. He stood still on the steps, waiting for his eyes to adjust. Tommy made it to the bottom without incident, he didn't fall and he didn't get shot, so things looked like they'd be OK. Objects started to come into focus in the dim light. Joe stepped down and stood behind Tommy. "Hello?" he said again and walked around Tommy into the main room. Sitting by a kerosene lamp was an old couple. "Hey, folks. Hope you don't mind if we join you."

"Sit on down," the farmer offered, "if the floor suits you. Sorry we don't have any chairs."

Joe laughed and then helped Tommy down to the floor, keeping them back in the shadows. "Thanks. My friend here, twisted his knee as we ran for the truck to get away from a funnel cloud we saw coming. We were driving by in our pickup and it started hailing again so we thought it best to get underground and saw your cellar doors."

"So, it's still pretty bad out there?" The farmer picked up his radio and turned it on. "We've been turning the radio on once in a while to listen. Trying to save the batteries since there's no power."

"There seems to be one storm front after another. We started driving after the first twister passed, but ran into another hailstorm. They say lightning doesn't strike twice, but I don't know if that applies to tornadoes."

The farmer nodded. "I stuck my head out and saw that everything's gone, so we decided to stay down here until we're sure it's safe to go out. We got what we need; some food and water for a while." The farmer's wife stayed silent and didn't make eye contact. She simply knitted, a bag at her feet with a string of yarn running up to her hands where she worked her knitting needles.

Joe looked around the cellar. The light from the kerosene lamp illuminating the walls which sparkled, the glass jars reflecting the light. His stomach rumbled. He took a step towards the shelves to inspect the jars. "Looks like you have some good stuff here; beets, corn, jam."

"The missus cans it. It's good."

Tommy's stomach growled and bubbled.

"Help yourself," the farmer said. "It sounds like you're hungry. I recommend the beets."

Joe plucked a jar off the shelf and tossed it to Tommy. He turned to the farmer to tell him he didn't like beets and saw him squint and study his clothes. Joe had stepped out of the shadows, his prison clothes visible in the light. They stared each other for a second, Joe tensed.

"Who are you boys?" the farmer asked. His wife looked up from her knitting, the clicking of the needles stopped.

"Everyone just stay calm," Joe said. He smiled at the farmer. He could see he was tense, his right arm poised to reach from something behind the box to his right. "We're just looking for a place to wait out this storm and then we'll be on our way."

The farmer's wife looked over the top of her glasses at Tommy. "You look familiar. You're that boy who killed that couple near North Platte, aren't you?"

Before Tommy could reply the farmer reached behind him. Joe stepped forward, catching site of the double-barreled shotgun in the farmer's grasp. He punched the farmer in the head and grabbed his arm. "I said stay calm!"

"Watch it!" Tommy yelled.

Joe felt a sharp pain in the back of his left leg. "Damn!" The pain was intense. He couldn't let go of the farmer's arm and let him get at the gun. He looked over his left shoulder and saw the farmer's wife pulling the knitting needles back to stab him again.

A jar flew the air and hit the woman in the head. She fell back onto her seat. "Bullseye." Tommy hopped over. "Don't move, bitch."

Joe wrenched the gun from the farmer's grasp, stepped back and pointed the gun at the farmer. He motioned with the gun barrel from the farmer towards his wife. "Go sit with her. I can cover you both with this scatter gun." He popped the gun open to check that both barrels had shells in them and snapped it shut again. "Shit, she stabbed me." Joe felt his leg. He brought his hand back up and inspected it in the light. "Bleeding a little bit, but not too bad. But God that hurt." He limped back a couple of steps. "Take this," he handed the shotgun to Tommy. "Watch them. I'm going to go check outside." He took a step towards the stairs. "Just watch them."

"Sure," Tommy answered.

JOE PUSHED OPEN the storm cellar door and looked outside. The wind and rain made it impossible to see very far. He could make out the pickup, but that was about. It. He lowered the doors and went down the stairs into the cellar.

"Well?" Tommy asked.

"Looks like we'll be staying a while. Still storming out. We might as well get some rest and eat up before we hit the road." Joe grabbed a couple of jars from the shelves and handed one to Tommy. "Hand me the gun. I'll take the first shift watching these two. You get some sleep."

THE CORN CRIB

The Blackhawk banked and circled the prison. Out the window, Ross saw the scar the tornado left across the landscape, one black line drawn across the fields right up to the prison walls and then it continued past the walls towards the northeast. The sky in the south looked like it was ready to spawn another beast at any time.

"Teams one and two ready to deploy," the command from Palmer through Ross' headset. "Team one, first in the southeast corner. Secure a position and report. Team two, Northeast corner. We'll set up base in the southwest. The Hawk may need to leave, depending on conditions. Good luck."

The helicopter lowered, the wheels just contacting the dirt and team one deployed. The sniper was out first, his support followed and the helicopter moved on to the second spot and repeated the maneuver. Then, they touched down in the southwest corner and the rest of the team deployed. Stevens, with Rupert muzzled and on his leash, took up a point outside of the rotor wash and stood sentry. Palmer strode over to the group huddled by some vehicles; prison staff, FBI field agents and the local sheriff. The rest of the team unloaded the Blackhawk. Supply lockers were color coded and stored separate from each other, ensuring that the team knew what was where, supporting their need for speed and efficiency.

Each team member checked their gear and stood in small groups, focused on the prison, talking through scenarios and assignments. Palmer rejoined the team. "Gentlemen, gather round." He keyed his mic. "Ground teams hear me?" He nodded and continued. "The storms have been constant here, just letting up an hour or so ago. One wing is back under the control of the prison. Two wings still need to be secured. There are prison worker hostages."

A field agent, wearing a windbreaker with FBI on the chest, walked up and handed Palmer some documents. He paged through them before continuing.

"Agent Fruen, two prisoners are missing from the west wing. Go see what you can learn." Palmer continued making assignments. "Stevens, you and Rupert hang here and see where you're needed. The rest of you, build us a model, scratch it on the ground, use boxes, whatever, get it ready and we'll assess next steps." He looked at Ross. "You still here? Go!"

Ross jogged to the entrance and asked for directions to the west wing. There he met a prison guard. "You have two inmates missing?"

"That's right. Follow me."

They climbed a set of stairs. At the top, the guard removed a set of keys and unlocked the steel door. It opened onto the roof. The guard relocked the door behind them and led Ross past some twisted conduits and piping. "Watch your step, it's a mess up here."

"What are we looking for?" Ross asked.

The guard led him past roof-top air conditioning units knocked off their mounts and over to the edge of the roof. Down below they could see the FBI team. In the distance, the plains of Nebraska stretched to the south. Straight ahead Ross could see the path a tornado left as it snaked across the ground, hit the prison and continued on its way. "And what are we looking for? Can you just spell it out? We're wasting time."

By the base of one air conditioning unit the guard bent over and pulled up a dirty blanket. "It's anchored here, I think they used it to climb down the wall." The guard stood and pointed south across the prairie. "And they walked away. They're out there somewhere."

Ross keyed his radio. "Boss, it's Fruen."

"Where are you?" Palmer asked.

"Look up." Ross waved at the group below.

"We don't have time for games, Agent Fruen. What have you discovered?"

"It looks like we have two prisoners who climbed down from here and escaped out through the gap in the fence. They're on the run."

Palmer waved and motioned him back. "Come on down. Looks like you, Stevens and Rupert have a job to do. Bring clothes or bedding from the escaped inmates cells. Maybe Rupert's part blood hound and can track them down."

"The Blackhawk is tied down because the weather is still

unstable and unpredictable. So, the two of you, I mean the three of you," Palmer dangled his hand down for Rupert to sniff, "will be driving that old Suburban."

Ross looked at the vehicle. Rusted quarter panels, two-toned, faded paint. How far could they get in it?

"Something wrong, Agent Fruen?" Palmer asked.

"No, sir."

"It doesn't look great, but it will get you where you need to get. Four-wheel drive, full tank of gas," he paused. "And you can't hurt it. It's already in bad shape. Two on the run wearing prison uniforms will stand out. But we don't have any idea which direction they went, so what are you going to do?"

Stevens held a plastic bag stuffed with cloth. "We've got some bedding, Rupert might be able to track them."

"And we'll stop at homes and businesses circling out from here to see if there's any sign of them or if people have anything unusual to report," Ross added.

"The warden has put out a report of two escaped inmates over the radio. And he's contacted immediate homes in the area, per their protocol. The first two homes or farms in each direction. Nobody has reported anything." Palmer handed some papers to Ross. "Here's a list of people they couldn't reach. Maybe not home, or phone's out or they're holed up in storm shelters. The map marks their locations. Start with them."

Ross unfolded the map and looked at it with Stevens. "Systematic and thorough until we find something or hear something," Ross said.

"We'll start here with Rupert since we know where they came down from the roof. See if he can pick up a scent," Stevens added.

Palmer tossed the keys and Ross snatched them out of

the air before Stevens could grab them. "You're Scarecrow, Stevens is Dorothy and that makes Rupert, Toto."

"Does that make you, the Wizard?" Ross asked.

Palmer laughed. "And this is Oz. We may not be in Kansas, but it all looks the same to me. Follow the yellow brick road, and bring back those flying monkeys. And bring back that Suburban."

STEVENS KNELT by the prison wall where they guessed the inmates had come down from the roof. He pulled some of the bedding out of the plastic bag for Rupert to smell. Rupert stuck his nose into the cloth. "Rupert, Zoeken." Stevens instructed.

Rupert looked up at the prison wall and then sniffed at the ground. He paced back and forth along the wall and then headed away from the prison. His nose in the dirt, tail in the air and his front paws stepping on either side of his nose. "Braaf," Stevens praised him. "Rupert, Zoeken." Stevens and Ross followed Rupert as he serpentined ahead of them, following a scent only he could smell.

RUPERT STOPPED in the middle of the road and looked around. He put his nose to the ground, and sniffed while he circled in a ten foot circle around some invisible spot on the road. "Looks like he's lost the scent here," Stevens said.

Ross looked back towards the prison, guessed they were about a quarter of a mile out, and then looked back down to the road they were standing on. "Somebody in a vehicle stopped to pick them up?"

"Or they flagged somebody down and took their vehicle."

"I'll go back and get our ride. Why don't you see what else Rupert might find."

NEBRASKA SAND HILLS

Joe stretched and turned his head, working the crick out of his neck. He had a smile on his face. He'd been dreaming of the beach and a woman with long, black hair, a señorita in a bikini. He opened his eyes and took a second to acclimate himself. He wasn't in his cell, he was in the storm cellar. He looked quickly to Tommy to make sure he was awake and then at the old couple. "How long have I been out?"

"I don't know," Tommy answered. "Maybe a couple hours. They know we've escaped. It was on the radio."

Standing up, Joe stretched his hands up and touched the ceiling. "Then we better get going. It sounds like the storm's let up outside. I'm going to go check it out."

It was cloudy, but it wasn't raining. Joe walked through the mud, climbed into the truck and turned the key. The engine turned over, but failed to start. "Come on, baby," Joe pleaded with the truck. He counted to five and turned the key again, while softly pressing a couple of times on the accelerator. "Come on." The truck turned over and then started with a roar. "Yes," Joe said to no one. He left the truck running and headed to the open hatch of the storm cellar to get Tommy.

One blast echoed from the open hatch. Joe, surprised, took a step back. A second blast echoed and Joe saw a flash of light. "Tommy!" With three quick steps he was at the open hatch. "Tommy, you OK?" Joe grabbed the hatch, ready to slam it shut.

Tommy peeked out from below. Smoke from the shots swirled in the light around him. "I'm OK."

"What the hell happened?"

"I heard the truck start and decided we couldn't leave witnesses behind."

Joe was quiet, thinking about options and how this could hurt or help them. "OK, it's done. Come on out. Bring the gun and the shells."

Tommy limped up the steps and hobbled over to the truck. Joe followed to help him into the bed. He looked in the back. It was empty. "Where's the body, Tommy?"

"I threw him out while we were driving down the road yesterday. He stunk."

"Where?"

"Not long after we got in the truck."

Tommy was so unpredictable. Joe squeezed the gun in his grasp and considered blasting Tommy and leaving him behind. "Let's go." He put the shotgun in the cab of the pickup. "I'll be right back."

Joe stood in the cellar. The farmer and his wife were on the bench where he'd last seen them. The farmer died trying to protect his wife, his body shielding her, a blast wound apparent in his back. Joe grabbed a basket and loaded it with canning jars. Then he picked up the kerosene lamp and climbed the steps. Outside he turned and tossed the lamp into the cellar. The fire would hide the scene below from any searchers. He put the basket in the pickup bed with Tommy. Black smoke started to pour out of the cellar doors. "Mehico, here we come."

Ross and Stevens sat in the idling Suburban. Two farms checked and no leads. On the radio they were listening to a weather report *"this is Hugh Hancock with a weather report. The storms that hit our region yesterday are followed by another front. Doppler radar indicates a number of hot spots, one includes the same area by the prison that got hit yesterday. Stay alert with your eyes on the sky and your radio tuned here for further updates."*

"You ever seen a tornado?" Stevens asked.

"No, but I've always wanted to. Something about the power from nature, the mystery of the spinning winds," Ross looked up at the skies. "Guess that's what gets those storm chasers out driving across tornado alley every season, trying to figure out the mystery."

"That, or they're just a little crazy." Stevens said. They both laughed.

"Why do you think they sent the two new guys out together? To get us out of their hair or as a test?" Ross asked.

Stevens looked out the open window. "Probably partly a test. I think for me, for us," he pointed at Rupert, "out in the open is a good assignment. We're used to operating out in the country."

"And me?" Ross asked.

"You know the FBI, procedures, law enforcement, operating in a city. I think we're a good team together. We can learn something from each other."

"Yeah, you're probably right." Ross looked out the window. "Palmer may know what he's doing."

The gravel road ahead of them split; two farms down the left branch, one down the right.

"Which way?" Ross asked. "Flip a coin?"

Stevens pulled out his binoculars and looked over the country side to the left, then the right. "I see some smoke this way." He pointed and handed the binoculars to Ross. "It's a sign of something. I say we go check that out first."

"We'll be able to see better from up there." About thirty yards out in the grass prairie, past a barbed wire fence, stood a windmill with a metal trough at its base for watering cattle. "How tall do you think it is, forty feet?"

"About that. Think it's sturdy after the storm?" Stevens asked.

"It's still standing." Ross climbed out of the truck. "Rock, paper, scissors to see who goes up?"

They stood in the ditch for their contest. "Three and throw," Ross said. He counted it down, pounding his right hand into his left palm. On the third he kept his fist closed. Stevens' right hand showed two fingers.

"Damn it." Stevens looked up at the windmill and swallowed. "I don't really like heights. Watch Rupert."

Ross laughed. "You don't like heights? Haven't you jumped out of planes? We flew here in the chopper."

"I'll do it. I don't have to like it."

"I'll climb it. Winner's choice. I kind of like heights." Ross stepped over to the windmill and looked up.

"Thanks. I owe you one. I'll let Rupert stretch his legs."

Ross grabbed onto the corner post and tried to shake the windmill. It seemed sturdy. A cross brace ran at an angle from one corner post to another. The metal was rough and pitted from years of standing sentinel over the Nebraska prairie, blasted by dirt blown during summer storms and frozen in numerous winters. He grabbed it with his gloved hand, stepped onto it and started to climb and shimmy up the braces to the top.

From the top, Ross could see pretty well in all directions. He pulled his binoculars out and looked towards the smoke. A farm, or what was left of one was the source. Smoke looked like it was coming from out of the ground.

"Hey, Fruen, come on down." Stevens yelled up.

Ross looked down at Stevens. "I think we should go check out that smoke, there's a farm there," he pointed in the direction of the smoke.

Stevens waved him down. "Yeah, after I show you something."

Ross climbed down the windmill. "Where's Rupert?"

"He's over in the ditch guarding a body." Stevens started walking away. "I'll show you."

"THINK THE TORNADO DUMPED HIM HERE?" Ross asked.

"From where?" Stevens turned around in a circle. "There's nothing out here?"

Stevens and Ross stood back, looking at the body on the ground. The man was definitely dead. His head angled unnaturally from the rest of the body. He was dressed in jeans and a dirty, white t-shirt. The shirt was pulled up exposing the white skin of his belly.

Stevens walked back along the road. "I think he was left here. Maybe thrown out of a car driving down the road." He pointed at a few skid marks in the gravel. "Bounced and tumbled and ended up where he is?"

Ross pulled out his GPS unit and marked the spot. Then he took some pictures with his phone to document what they'd found. "Can't wait for the medical examiner. Check the body for ID?"

Stevens knelt by the body and checked the pockets. "No wallet, but I have a receipt here." He held it out in his hand, Ross captured an image of it with his camera.

"Can't read the signature. But they should be able to ID it from the credit card number." He shook his head. "Still no cell signal." He pulled out the satellite phone and called Palmer.

Ross pulled the Suburban into the farm yard. Smoke billowed out of the ground through a storm cellar door. Laying outside of the door was a person. Ross stopped the vehicle next to the body and hopped out. Stevens and Rupert exited the other side of the vehicle, keeping it between them and the cellar door. Stevens eyed the storm cellar, his MP5 in his hands, ready to shoot. Rupert took his command and circled the site in a bigger arc. "Ross?" Stevens questioned over the roof of the vehicle.

"She's dead." Ross answered. He knelt down next to the body. She was an older woman, her skirt was partly burned. Her right shoulder, chest area was ripped open. "Looks like she was shot."

Rupert sniffed at the ground and sat. "They were here," Stevens said. "He's picked up their scent around here. Must've walked from the cellar to a vehicle."

"We're on the right track. At least we know we're going the right direction," Ross said. "They're armed."

The smoke was thinning with the fire burning itself out underground. Ross collected debris from the area around the foundation and covered the woman's body to provide it some protection from birds or animals roaming the area, until the sheriffs could get there to recover the bodies.

Their radios crackled. "Scarecrow and Dorothy, this is Oz. We've got an ID on the vehicle you're looking for. Ran the card you gave us and found who it belonged to and what he drove."

"Go ahead, Oz," Ross answered.

"It's a red Ford pickup. 1984."

"Any idea where it is?" Ross asked.

"No, but now you know what you're looking for."

"Oz, any chance of sending up a drone to scan the area for it?"

"Negative, not with this weather, and the closest one is in Omaha. Keep searching. We've got an addendum to the radio report on the escapees adding the vehicle to the watch, maybe we'll get lucky from an alert citizen."

"Oz, we've got another body, maybe two." Ross gave him the GPS coordinates.

"That's enough bodies. Go find these guys. And be careful."

"We'll keep looking, out."

SANDHILLS PUMP & GO

Sandhills Pump and Go was a two-pump station with a garage stall for repairs. An old tow truck was parked out by the road, its faded sign advertising the station on the door.

Joe pulled into the gas station and parked on the far side of the pumps to keep them hidden from the attendant in the station. He stood next to the truck and spoke with Tommy. "The pump takes credit cards. Give me a card from the guy's wallet, keep an eye on the station for any weird stuff, and we'll get gassed up and out of here."

Tommy handed Joe the card, popped the gun open and loaded two shells in it.

The pump started, the dials slowly turned. "Damn these old stations," Joe said. "They never change out the fuel filters and gas dribbles out." He grabbed the handle, stopped the flow and squeezed the handle hard again. The flow didn't change. He could hear the gas flow through the hose and watched the numbers slowly spin. "Come on."

"Do we need to fill it full?" Tommy asked.

"As long as we can get out of here without being discovered, I want to be able to get as far as we can."

"If we're here much longer, I'm going to have to take a leak," Tommy joked.

"Just hold it until we get out of here. Then you can piss all over Nebraska." Joe tapped his toe and glanced at the station. They still hadn't seen anyone and no other cars had pulled into the station. He looked up at the sky. "Think the weather has passed?"

"No, look at those clouds. They're still green and ugly. I think we're just between fronts." Tommy said. "This is one monster storm."

The gas pump stopped.

Joe returned the gas handle to the pump, snatched another glance at the station and got in the pickup. "Looks like we lucked out here."

"Mehico, here we come," Tommy answered.

Joe turned the key. The engine turned over, but didn't start. He pumped the gas pedal a couple of times and turned the key again. The result was the same.

"Try it again. It was just running."

He took a deep breath, closed his eyes and turned the key. The engine turned over, but didn't start. Joe turned the key harder, in his frustration. "Damn it."

"Joe, somebody's coming."

An attendant in blue, oil-stained coveralls walked towards them. An oval patch over his heart read, "Bill" in red stitching on a white background. He had a rag in his hands, wiping them off as he walked. He spit a stream of brown juice onto the gravel lot. "Sounds like you've got some trouble," he said as he approached the vehicle. Then he suddenly stopped, about six feet from the front of the truck. He kept his hands in front of him. "Can I pop the hood and see if we can get this started and get you boys on your way?" His jaw twitched and he licked his lips.

"Tommy." Joe said.

Tommy stood in the back of the pickup and pointed the shotgun at the attendant.

"Now if you'd be so kind to walk around to the back of the truck I think it would be best to push it over behind your garage. Get it out of the way where you can work on it," Joe said.

"Sure. Sure, I can do that." He walked around the pumps to the back of the truck.

"Anyone else inside that could help us?" Joe asked.

"Nope. Just me. Too quiet out here to need anyone else."

Tommy sat down in the bed of the truck, the gun still aimed at the attendant.

"OK, then. I'll drive and you push." Joe said. "Let's go."

"Gentlemen, go get 'em."

"Where are they?" Stevens asked into his radio.

Palmer answered, "Your victim's credit card was just used to purchase gas about twenty minutes from where you are. At Sandhills Pump and Go. Ready for the coordinates?"

Ross held the GPS unit in his hand, his fingers poised to enter the numbers. "He's ready. Go," Stevens replied.

Ross typed in the numbers as Palmer recited them. He shifted the truck into drive. "They've got twenty minutes on us, but we know they're heading south. Nowhere else to go."

"Not a lot of roads around here."

"Let's go get 'em." Ross said.

JOE STOPPED with the pickup hidden around the side of the garage. "Can you get this started?"

The mechanic opened the hood as far as he could. It resisted with a screech as the old springs stretched and metal rubbed on metal. The bent hood and front panels prevented him from opening it all the way. "I'll see what I can do. If I can get you on your way will you let me be?"

Tommy stood behind him with the shotgun. "Just get it going. We need to hit the road."

From under the hood, the mechanic gave the order, "Try it now."

Joe turned the key and it turned over, but it didn't sound anywhere close to starting.

"I think the starter's fried," the mechanic said, from under the hood. "It's old and looks like you rolled it in the storm."

"Try it again," Joe ordered.

"OK, go," came the command from under the hood.

The results were the same. "Damn it." Joe climbed out of the truck. He looked out at the road, nobody was driving by. Couldn't carjack a vehicle. He turned to the mechanic, who had crawled out from under the hood and stood in front of the truck. "Can you fix it?"

"If I had another starter. But I don't"

"No vehicles in the service garage?"

The mechanic barked out a quick laugh. "One old car up on the rack I'm working on. But it's in worse shape than your truck."

Joe scanned the sky to give himself a chance to think. "How did you get to work today?"

"What?"

"How did you get here? What did you drive?"

"I didn't. My wife dropped me off."

"When's she coming back?"

"Well, usually around supper time. But with the weather and everything." The mechanic wiped his hands and didn't finish his thought.

"What?" Joe asked.

"Just thinking about my wife. Can't get a hold of her. Phone's out and cell service sucks out here." He wiped his hands again. "I'm sure she's fine. Probably be here with supper if the weather's not too bad."

"PULL OVER," Stevens said. "The station is up there on the left about a quarter mile."

Ross eased the Suburban onto the gravel shoulder.

Stevens studied the station through his binoculars. "Looks quiet. No activity."

"Let's drive by," Ross said. "We can either pull in, drive by and go back or keep going." Ross shifted the truck into drive and pulled onto the road.

"You're the boss."

The old service station was an oasis in the middle of the Nebraska sandhills. Scrubland with some brush clinging to it surrounded the station. The Sandhills Pump and Go sign flanked the highway with an old tow truck parked at its base. The gas pumps stood in the middle of the empty lot.

"Looks quiet," Ross said. He slowed the truck down to about forty miles per hour. "I don't see anybody."

They continued to roll past. "Hey, I see something. Keep going and then pull over." Stevens twisted in his seat to look back at the station. "Looks like our red pickup is parked on the side of the station."

Ross checked the rearview mirror. "See anyone?"

"Nobody outside."

"Let me know when you can't see the station anymore. Then I'll pull over." Ross kept up their speed and watched the station through the mirror.

Stevens had his binoculars trained on the station. Rupert looked back out the window in the direction he was looking. "OK, we should be good."

Ross checked over his shoulder and turned the truck in a U-turn. He stopped on the right shoulder, the nose of the truck pointed back towards the station. "We need eyes on the station. How about you and Rupert see what you can see and I'll stay here in case they head this way in the truck."

"Sounds good." Stevens stepped out of the Suburban and checked his gear. "We'll see what we can find out." He opened the back door, grabbed his HK Sniper Rifle and Rupert bounded out.

"Stay in touch so I know what's going on," Ross said. Stevens gave him a thumbs-up, then he and Rupert took off across the hard scrabble at a trot.

RAINDROPS SPATTERED the windshield of the Suburban; a few at first, then more, with increasing intensity. The country music playing on the radio got drowned out by the rain. Ross turned on the windshield wipers. They cleared the water, leaving a trail of streaks allowing him to see forward. He knew Stevens and Rupert were somewhere out there getting wet. "Dorothy, how are you and Toto doing?" Ross asked into the radio.

After a few seconds, Stevens answered. "We're circling around back. Think we made the wrong choice, choosing to come out. We're getting a little wet." There was another break, then Stevens continued, "Have you looked out your window to the southwest?"

Ross rolled down the window, rain sprinkled his face. "What the hell is that?" he radioed to Stevens.

"You said you've wanted to see the power of a tornado."

"I don't think that's your run of the mill tornado," Ross answered.

Gray clouds had formed into a gigantic circle, like a giant yoyo spinning on its side in the sky. It was hard to tell how far away it was or exactly what direction it was going. But wherever it went, it was going to cause some destruction.

On the radio Hugh Hancock interrupted the country music, "*residents of Thompson County, if you haven't looked outside, don't. Head to your basements and shelters. A giant Supercell has formed as the warm and cold fronts we were watching have come together. It appears to be following the same path of yesterday's storm. Sit tight, stay indoors and stay safe.*"

"Dorothy. I just got a weather report from our friend on the radio. I think we may want to seek the safety of that building. The storm is coming this way. And it's a big one."

Stevens answered, "We'll see what we can see, but if they're inside we may need a new plan."

THE PRAIRIE PLAYED tricks on his ability to judge how far away the storm was. Ross wiped the rain from his face and stared at the clouds, trying to judge their distance and direction. The wind picked up in intensity and he saw a wall of rain marching in his direction. "Stevens. The storm is almost here. I'm rolling towards the station."

Stevens answered. "Rupert and I will meet you there.

We're heading towards the rear of the station. Don't dawdle. The tornado is on your tail."

Dawdle? Where'd that word come from, Ross thought? He turned on the headlights, took off his helmet and drove toward the station.

ROSS PARKED next to the pumps, the driver's door away from the station. In the rain he couldn't see anything at the station, so they wouldn't be able to see him either. "I can't see anything from here. How about you?"

"I'm not in position where I can see them through the scope yet," Stevens answered. "Give me another thirty seconds."

"Roger, don't dawdle." Ross smiled.

"My name's not Roger," Stevens replied.

Ross laughed to himself. Keeping things loose to release some of the tension, that was a good sign. He looked again at the station. He couldn't just sit here too long. He looked back at the storm front that was closing in on them as well. Rain continued to fall pounding on the roof and hood of the Suburban.

JOE LOOKED out the rain spattered window at the Suburban parked at the gas pump. "Bill, do you recognize that truck?"

Bill glanced out the window. "Nope. Not one of my regulars."

"You can tell that quick?"

"I don't have that many customers. I know them all by name and vehicle," Bill said, pronouncing the H in vehicle.

"He's not getting out," Tommy said, as he limped nervously, pointing the shotgun out towards the lot.

Joe gazed out the window. "Could be our ride out of here, Tommy. It's old, but it's in better shape than our pickup."

Joe grabbed Bill's shoulder. "Make it so he can't pay at the pump. We need him to come inside."

Bill shuffled over to the register and pushed a couple of buttons. "I set it to prepay inside, they'll see the message on the pump."

"He's just sitting there, Joe. He's not getting out." Tommy peered out the window from around the corner.

"Maybe waiting for the rain to let up." Joe pushed Bill down into a chair. "We'll wait, but not too long. We need him to come in or we're going to have to go out and get that truck."

"FRUEN, need to find cover. That's a big ass storm and it's almost here."

The rain intensified it's pounding on the Suburban and the wind was starting to rock the vehicle on its old shocks. "My vote is the service bay on the end of the station. Just a small window, big service door, solid walls except for the service door and maybe a mechanics pit under a car hoist." Ross peered towards the station. "I still don't see anyone inside"

"Rupert and I are heading for the back door of the garage. Time for some entry and cover."

Ross could hear the storm, the jostling of the equipment and the heavy breathing of Stevens as he ran across the field. Stevens was in the open. Ross hoped he'd make it to the garage before the storm. He had to get there himself. He turned on the headlights and shifted the Suburban into gear.

"JOE. Shit. He's getting ready to go."

"What?"

"He just turned his lights on. I think he's getting ready to go." Tommy shifted his weight from foot to foot, favoring his good leg.

"Damn it. Watch Bill." Joe ran for the door. He reached out for the shotgun as he passed Tommy, grabbed it and burst out the door at a run.

Outside, the wind and rain pelted his face. He swiped it away with his free hand as he ran for the truck. He couldn't let it get away. It started to roll forward.

"Stop!" he yelled. He grabbed the shotgun in both hands ready to fire if they didn't stop.

THE GARAGE WAS BEHIND ROSS. He had to swing around and get to the door, enter and meet Stevens. A tumbleweed blew across the lot through the headlight beams, bouncing off into the open prairie. The signs by the gas pumps vibrated in the wind. The storm was coming.

They had two objectives; get out of the storm and capture the fugitives. Ross glanced to his right and saw the silhouette of someone running towards him. The light from the station windows showed the silhouette of a man with a rifle or shotgun in his hands. Ross punched the accelerator, the rear wheels spun, spitting gravel and then caught, launching him forward. He cranked the steering wheel to the right and the back end fishtailed pointing him towards the garage. The headlights caught a figure standing with a shotgun pointed at him.

Ross ducked to his right and pushed the accelerator to the floor. There was a loud roar and the windshield imploded. Shattered safety glass covered his lap and rain was falling in through the hole in the windshield. He chanced a peek over the dash. The garage door was ahead of him. Crash into the door to gain entry and protection? Stop short of the door, protect himself with his sidearm and see if the service door was open, if not kick it in? He glanced back to see if the man with the shotgun was following.

The back window was blown out by another blast from the shotgun. Ross swerved the truck and ran it into the garage door. He scrambled across the seat to exit from the passenger door to keep the Suburban between him and the shooter.

"Stevens, I'm taking fire. One shooter."

"Almost there."

Ross grabbed the handle of the passenger door and opened it.

The wind ripped it from his grasp and flung it to the limit of its hinges. It rebounded closed and crushed Ross' arm. "Damn."

He pushed the door open and stepped out of the truck and looked through the window at the shooter. His right hand was numb and he couldn't grab his gun from the holster.

The shooter pushed another couple of shells into the shotgun. Ross saw him approaching the Suburban. He reached for his sidearm with his left hand and struggled to pull the gun from the holster. "Stevens, where are you?"

"Approaching the back of the station."

The wind was increasing. Ross' ears popped with a change in the pressure.

A blur as something blew past him. Another tumbleweed?

There was another blast and flash from the shotgun and the tumbleweed flew into the gunman.

It wasn't a tumbleweed, it was Rupert.

JOE LINED up the barrel of the shotgun on the cop hiding on the other side of the truck. A couple of windows gone, but it was drivable. It was their way out of here. He took a step to his right, into the wind. Sand and rain struck the right side of his face, but he maintained his focus on the cop. He started to pull the trigger and boom, something ran into his side, knocking him to the ground.

The shotgun went off when he hit the ground. What the hell? What hit him?

Joe heard a growl and scrambled to his feet. The beast lunged at him again. He didn't have time to aim and fire, so he swung the stock of the shotgun around like a home run swing to hit the animal. It yelped. Joe stumbled from the blow. The strong winds just about pushed him over. Joe limped back to the station to get out of the storm and away from whatever attacked him.

ROSS RAISED up to cover Rupert. The assailant walked through the door of the service station. Rupert was gone.

"Stevens, I'm still in front of the garage. We need to take cover. The storm's getting worse."

Stevens responded in his ear piece, "I'm coming around the corner of the garage. Don't shoot me."

"You're clear."

Stevens joined Ross next to the Suburban, rocking on its suspension from the wind. Rain and sand blew into them. "They're in the station. We need to get in the garage quick, before they head there for protection from this storm," Ross said. "I'll go first, see what we've got for protection from the storm and those guys."

"Make it quick." Stevens aimed at the door of the station. "I'll make sure they don't come out this door. How about Rupert?"

"The guy outside hit him with the stock of the gun when Rupert knocked him down. I think he's OK, but I didn't see where he went."

Stevens nodded. "I lost my comm-link with him. We'll find him when this is through. You better go."

Ross slid over the hood of the truck and squatted by the tire. The garage door was pushed off the tracks, but it would be a tight squeeze through into the garage. He tried the man-door first. The knob turned. Not locked. Would it swing open? One step at a time, Ross told himself.

Joe stumbled into the station.

"What the hell, Joe?"

"We have company, Tommy, and it's not some farmer." Joe pointed the shotgun at the door. "At least one guy and a dog."

"What are we going to do?"

"The storm's getting bad. We survive that in this box and maybe we find a chance to get out of here. Their truck is smashed into the garage door, but it was running." Joe motioned Bill up with the muzzle of the shotgun. "Help

Tommy flip this desk over. We'll hide behind this and the back wall."

Tommy and Bill flipped the big metal desk on its side. "Why don't we go in the garage?" Bill asked. "It'll be safer."

"That's where they're going."

"I thought you said there was only one." Tommy said.

"That's all I saw. I would've had him too, if the dog didn't attack me." Joe walked around the desk and slid down into a sitting position, his back against the block wall. Rain, sand and other debris slammed into the windows facing the front of the service station. "You guys better get back here before those windows give." He kept the shotgun aimed at Bill.

Ross pushed the door open, slowly swinging it inward on its hinges. The wind ripped the knob from his grasp and it flew open, slamming into the wall. A quick peek around the door into the garage. Nobody shot at him. He entered in a crouch and sidestepped further into the garage. He keyed his mic. "Clear. I'm moving to the back wall away from the office. I'll cover the door."

From one knee, Ross kept his gun aimed at the door. Stevens entered and backpedaled to join him. The garage door rattled on its rails, the bent in corner started to peel a little further open.

"Into the pit," Stevens ordered. "That tornado's going to hit and we need the protection."

They both slithered into the grease pit below the car that was being serviced in the garage. Stevens covered the door to the station. "We've got great coverage here from the storm and from those guys."

"Where's Rupert?" Ross asked.

"He'll find cover." Stevens replied. "He's smarter than the two of us put together.

The garage door rattled and Ross felt the pressure change in his ears.

"Hey," he yelled. "We're the FBI! The storm's going to hit any second. Come in with your arms up and you can join us here in the garage!" He waited for an answer. None came. "You're not going to make it sitting in a glass box!"

THE MAIN DOOR of the service station flew open on its hinges, sucked out by the pressure. Papers flew around the office and rain, dirt and other debris flew in.

"Fuck!" Joe jumped behind the desk with Tommy and Bill just as one of the main windows imploded sending glass flying and more rain and debris into the station.

"Now what?" Tommy yelled to be heard above the wind.

"Ride this out and see what's next," Joe replied.

Bill curled up in the fetal position with his arms wrapped around his head.

Joe handed the shotgun to Tommy. "Keep the Feds out of here and use Bill as a hostage if you need to."

"What are you doing?" Tommy asked.

Wind and dirt continued to blow in through the open door and blown out window.

"It seems like the tornado's passed. It'll get quiet fast. I'm going to see if their truck works." Joe jumped up and limped out through the front blown out window.

OUTSIDE, he leaned into the the wind. The Suburban was still running as it rested against the garage door. If he was careful, he could make it to the truck and get in without alerting the Feds in the garage. He hopped and limped as quick as he could to the open door of the truck and climbed into the driver's seat.

Gas looked good, enough to get away. If he was going to go, now was the time. The Feds would be busy with Tommy and wouldn't have a vehicle. He shifted into reverse and gunned it. There was a shriek of metal as the truck disengaged from the door. "Sorry, Tommy!" Joe yelled as he executed a quick half circle, braked and slammed the transmission into drive.

"Ross, somebody's taking off in the truck."

"Let's secure the office and then we'll take care of the truck." Ross walked towards the door, his back sliding against the cement block wall for protection as he approached. "FBI! Anybody in the office, put your hands above your head!"

A voice called back from inside the station office. "Stay back! I have a hostage in here."

"Listen," Ross said. "Your buddy left you behind. Give yourself up, and let the hostage go."

Stevens quietly headed for the hole torn in the garage door when the truck pulled away. Ross signaled that he'd keep talking and for Stevens to circle around to the other side of the station.

"I can't do that man. I can't go back to the Crib. I got nothing to lose here now."

"Are you Martinelli or Kelly?"

"That fucker, Joe, left me behind man. What the fuck?"

Ross eased a little closer to the door, but made sure he stayed out of site. "Hey, listen. You've had your little adventure outside the prison. Got to see a tornado close up. But, now it's time to end this. Give up, we'll catch up with Joe and you can have a little heart to heart about him leaving you behind."

"No, you listen! I want a vehicle here that I can use. My friend, Bill here, will drive until I'm sure we're not followed and then I'll let him go, unharmed. Anything funny happens, I'll shoot him."

Ross whispered into his mic, "Stevens, he's sounding a little desperate here. Tell me when you're set up. I'll leave my mic open so you can hear our conversation."

"Give me thirty seconds to get in position and another ten to get set up." Ross could here Stevens breathing heavy and his equipment rattling as he hustled to get into position.

"Martinelli. Think about this. Nobody needs to get hurt. We end this here and now and we get you back to your comfortable cell. Then we go get Joe." Ross moved right up to the edge of the door into the office with his back against the wall. "Where were you guys headed to?"

"None of your business."

"Bill, are you OK?" Ross asked.

"Yep. I'm OK."

"I'm set," Ross heard Stevens say in his headset.

"Martinelli, I'm going to stand in the doorway here so I can see how Bill is doing and we can talk." Ross hung the HP from it's sling and slowly slid into the doorway with his hands in the air. "I'm Special Agent Fruen with the FBI. Let's stay calm and talk this through."

Tommy shoved the end of the shotgun firmly into Bill's back and Bill grimaced.

"Martinelli, relax," Ross said.

"I don't think he's giving up," Stevens said. "I've got him in my sights, but the hostage is too close."

"We can do this the easy way or the hard way, Martinelli. What do you say?"

"I told you I want a ride out of here," Tommy yelled.

"You from Nebraska, Bill?" Ross asked. Bill nodded. "How about you?" Ross looked at Martinelli. He nodded.

Ross went on. "My roommate and I were talking about how people talk different, refer to things differently depending on where they're from." Ross lowered his hands and leaned into the doorframe, relaxing.

"Where you going with this, Ross?" Stevens asked.

"Here you drink red beer, maybe call the interstate the freeway. My roommate has an accent and calls every soft drink a Coke. It's ridiculous." Ross paused to see if Tommy and Bill were listening. Tommy looked at Bill's back and Ross winked at Bill.

"Or there's kids' games. We called it Duck, Duck, (he winked at Bill) Gray Duck," Ross emphasized the last Duck and swung his HP on its sling up into a shooting position. Bill dropped to the floor, leaving Tommy exposed. Stevens fired and Ross followed with a shot to the chest. Tommy fell back into the wall and then slumped to the floor, the shotgun still in his grasp.

Ross quickly stepped over and grabbed the shot gun. "Clear," he reported to Stevens over the radio.

"You shot me," screamed Martinelli.

Stevens entered, gun drawn. "What's up? He's alive?"

"I think your bullet grazed his shoulder. My shot hit his arm."

"I was aiming for his head. He moved when he dropped," Stevens nodded at Bill.

"I was aiming center mass. You want to see if you can patch him up while I cover him?"

Bill remained seated on the floor where he'd dropped. "Are you OK?" Ross asked.

Bill nodded.

"I'm glad you understood where I was going with my story." Ross reached down and offered Bill some help up from the floor. "Let's get you seated in this chair and check you out." Ross swept debris off the chair and helped Bill sit. "You're the only one here, right?"

"Yep, this is my place." Bill looked around the inside of the station. Windows were gone, water, dirt, plants and gravel covered the floor and any surface. "Guess we survived the tornado."

"Yes we did," Ross said. "Anyone we can call for you?"

Bill shook his head. "The wife's at home, but I think the phones are out."

"Just glad you were paying attention," Ross said. "We still have one on the run."

"Maybe not," Stevens said.

"What do you mean?"

"I looked down the road before I came in. The Suburban's off the road about a half mile from here."

Ross checked to see if the shotgun was loaded. "Can you handle a shotgun, Bill?"

"I've hunted birds."

"Just in case he comes back." Ross handed the shotgun to Bill. "We're going to head down the road to the Suburban."

"I don't think they had any other guns. I just saw the shotgun."

"Well, just in case," Ross said.

"Sir, you going to be OK while we go check out our car down the road?" Stevens asked. "I handcuffed this one to the desk, so he shouldn't bother you."

"I'm not going anywhere," Bill said.

Ross and Stevens started jogging down the road. Spread out. One on either shoulder of the road.

After about fifty yards they stopped. Stevens raised his rifle and looked through the scope. He laughed.

"What?" Ross asked.

"You were wondering what happened to Rupert." Stevens crossed the road and handed his rifle to Ross.

Ross looked through the scope. The Suburban was stopped against a telephone pole on the far side of the right ditch. He moved the scope to the left and chuckled. "That's quite the partner you have there." Kelly was on the ground with Rupert clamped down on his arm. "We better go back up your partner."

Joe Kelly lie on the ground. Rupert's jaws were clamped around his left, upper arm. He softly repeated his growl anytime Joe moved.

"God damn it, get this dog off of me!"

"Joe Kelly, we're FBI agents Fruen and Stevens. You've met Agent Rupert."

"Can you get this dog off me? It hurts!"

Stevens stepped over to Rupert and tapped him on the left haunch. "Rupert, Braaf."

Rupert kept his grip on Joe's arm. "Joe, I'm going to release the dog. You're not going to move. I will approach you and ask you to put your arms behind your back. Then I will handcuff you."

"OK," Joe mumbled.

Ross moved to the other side of Joe Kelly to keep him covered in case he tried to get away.

"Put your right arm behind your back," Stevens ordered Kelly. After putting one cuff on Kelly's right wrist he issued an order to Rupert, "Rupert, Laat Los."

Rupert released Joe's arm and remained standing in position, on alert.

"Joe, slowly put your left wrist behind your back." Stevens handcuffed his other wrist and issued another order. "Rupert, Erop."

"All good?" Ross asked.

Stevens pulled his sidearm from his holster. "Rupert and I have him covered. Why don't you check out the Suburban."

Ross scanned the skies. It was still cloudy, but not so menacing. Joe was seated on the ground with Rupert a foot or two behind him, periodically barking.

"Doesn't sound like it's going to start." Stevens said.

"Nope. Our friend here drove it into the pole hard enough to do some damage." Ross stepped over to Joe and asked, "What happened?"

Joe looked up at Ross. "I was driving down the road, thought I was getting away." He shook his head. "Then I heard a growl from the back seat. I glanced in the rearview mirror and saw this monster flying over the seat from the back end. I reacted. Cranked the wheel I guess and swerved, bounced through the ditch and hit the pole. He flew into the dash and I bailed out. I didn't get far, when I felt him attack. Every time I moved or hit him he dug in tighter and pulled on my arm, so I tried to play dead. That's where you found me."

Ross looked and Stevens. "Let's hoist him up and walk back to the station. See if we can call for a ride."

They stood on either side and helped him to his feet.

"Can I get this arm treated?" Kelly asked.

"You'll be fine," Stevens answered. "Some punctures, maybe a few tears. We'll have the prison doc take a look at you."

"How's Tommy?"

Ross answered. "He's pissed at you for leaving him behind."

"OK, Joe," Stevens said. "You lead us back to the station. Rupert will be right behind you and we'll be behind him. You try to run and you have a pretty good idea of what's going to happen."

Kelly started walking down the highway towards the station.

Stevens barked an order, "Rupert, Transport."

Rupert closely followed Kelly down the road, barking and growling to keep him moving ahead.

"You know, if we're going to be partners," Ross said, "you need to teach me some of these orders."

"Yeah, we'll see," Stevens said.

THE FOUR OF them walked across the gravel lot towards the gas station. Ross yelled out, "Bill, we're coming in. Don't shoot."

Bill walked out of the station.

"Can you hand me the gun?" Stevens asked.

Bill handed it over. "I wouldn't shoot him," Bill said.

Ross patted Bill on the shoulder as he passed him. "Yeah, we know. Just need to be safe."

"Joe, we're going to have you sit while we figure out what

we're going to do next." Stevens said. "Rupert, Zit." Rupert quickly sat. "OK Joe, sit down."

Joe bent his legs and kind of fell onto his side and then sat up.

"Rupert, Erop."

"I got Zit is sit, but what was the other order?" Ross asked.

"Erop." Stevens lightly rolled the R. "It means to guard. He's going to watch over Joe until I release him and give him another command."

"Alright, let's figure out what we're going to do next," Ross said. "We got the two escapees. Wrecked our transportation. I don't see any other cars here." He looked at Bill. "Any ideas?"

"Betty runs," Bill said.

"Betty?" Stevens asked.

"Betty," Bill said and pointed out at the tow truck. "My tow truck. She runs."

"What?" Joe said. "That piece of shit runs? I thought it was your advertisement for your station. You said you didn't have any other vehicles."

"Well, I don't drive it much and forgot about her."

"Will she make it back to the prison?" Ross asked.

Bill scratched his chin. "Sure, once I get her started. Just don't drive too fast."

"We're not all going to fit in her," Stevens said.

Ross smiled. "Bill, get her started. We'll figure it out."

THE CORN CRIB

They pulled up to the prison; Ross driving, Stevens in the passenger seat and Rupert seated between them. Smoke billowed from the exhaust pipe. When they got to the HRT command post, Ross braked and rolled down the window.

"What's this?" Palmer asked.

Ross got out of the tow truck. "You said to bring back the Suburban."

"In one piece," Palmer said. Are the prisoners in better shape?"

"They're in the Suburban. One in the back seat. One in the front. They're not really getting along," Ross said.

"And they should probably see a doctor," Stevens added.

Ross unchained Martinelli from the steering wheel and got him out of the driver's seat. "Tommy here, suffered a gunshot. Or a couple. One went through, and the other grazed him."

Stevens and Rupert walked Kelly around from the other side of the Suburban. "And Kelly here has a dog bite on his arm that should be looked at."

Palmer semi-smiled and put his hands on his hips. "Nice job for three rookies on their first assignment together. Get them over to the prison and checked in with the guards there. We're wrapping things up and heading home. The prison staff has things under control and the Omaha FBI office is here to tie things up. I want to get out of here before it gets dark."

Ross pet Rupert on top of his head and looked at Stevens. "Can I try?"

"I thought you didn't like dogs." Stevens said.

"He's growing on me."

"Give her a shot."

Ross grabbed Martinelli and Kelly and pointed them towards the prison. Then he stepped back and gave the order, "Rupert. Transport."

Rupert barked and nosed the back of Kelly's leg.

Kelly cringed and yelled, "We're going!"

Ross threw his bag on his bed. "Oh man, I'm beat."

"How long have we been gone?" Stevens asked. "What time is it?"

"I don't know for sure. Which time zone? Maybe after a shower and some sleep I'll be thinking a little clearer."

There was a knock on the door. "Showers needs to wait, gentlemen. Palmer wants to see you in the shoot house. All three of you."

PALMER WAS STANDING at the door waiting for them. "Follow me."

Ross, Stevens and Rupert followed Palmer into the shoot house. The room was dark. Rupert let out a low growl.

"Rupert, Vrij," Stevens commanded.

"What's that mean?" Ross asked.

"At ease."

They stood in the dark for a couple of seconds and then the lights came on. All the members of A team were there, cheering. Rupert barked.

Palmer handed a beer to Ross and to Stevens and motioned for the team to quiet down. "I want to congratulate you all on a successful mission." He raised his bottle in the air. "And to welcome the new members of our team, agents Fruen, Stevens and Rupert."

Team members clinked their bottles together and drank.

Ross and Stevens did the same. "Congrats," Ross said.

"You too."

Palmer walked over. "I hope you enjoyed working together. I think we'll team you up on the next mission too."

Ross took another swig of his beer. "Only if he teaches me some more of those Dutch commands."

Stevens smiled. "We'll work on it."

THANKS FOR READING

SuperCell is the first novella in the FBI Hostage Rescue Team, Critical Incident series. It's born as a spin off from my first FBI Thriller – The Ninth District, where Special Agent Ross Fruen is introduced as a secondary character.

If you haven't read The Ninth District yet, join the Dorow Thriller Reader list and you can get it for FREE.

If you enjoyed this book, one way to show it and support my writing is to leave a review at your favorite online bookstore.

Read for the THRILL of it!

AFTERWORD

People ask where I get my ideas. The idea for SuperCell - Critical Incident #1 is a mashup.

When I finished writing The Ninth District, I got some good feedback on Agent Ross Fruen from my writing group and people wondered what was going to happen to him. I decided to create a spin-off series, starting with SuperCell following Agent Ross Fruen as he joined the FBI's Hostage Rescue Team (HRT), a kind of elite SWAT unit deployed on special cases related to anti-terrorism and other crimes where local law enforcement needs the help of a team with special skills.

The idea for SuperCell itself came after I heard a news story about a jail getting hit by a tornado and some prisoners escaped. I upped the ante so I could bring in the HRT.

Rupert was in the story since I started writing it, but got some additional details after I attended the Writers Police Academy the summer of 2016. One demonstration was by a sheriff's deputy who had a canine partner specializing in searching for explosives. As he demonstrated the search around a car where he had hidden a container containing a small amount of explosives, he gave some funny sounding commands to his dog. We learned that a lot of the service dogs are trained in Dutch. I decided to bring that into the story.

I try to bring reality to my stories. I attended the Minneapolis FBI Citizens Academy in 2015 and the Writers Police Academy in 2016.

One important tip I heard at the WPA; I was talking to a woman who is a co-writer with James Patterson. She said she told Patterson that she was going to attend the Writers Police Academy. He said that was fine, but remember, "don't let the facts get in the way of our fiction".

I want to make my stories real enough to be believable while remaining entertaining.

For my family and the agents and staff of the FBI.

ABOUT THE AUTHOR

Douglas "Doug" Dorow, lives in Minneapolis, Minnesota with his wife, two children and their dogs. SuperCell is his second book.

He is a graduate of the Minneapolis FBI Citizens Academy - 2015 and the Writers' Police Academy 2016.

For more info on my writing:

www.douglasdorow.com
Doug@DouglasDorow.com

ALSO BY DOUGLAS DOROW

The Ninth District - FBI Thriller #1

SuperCell - Critical Incident #1

www.douglasdorow.com for more info:

For updates on new releases, exclusive promotions and other information, sign up for Douglas Dorow's Thriller Reader list

Sign up now and get THE NINTH DISTRICT, the FBI thriller that started it all.

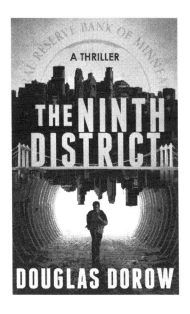

Made in the USA
Monee, IL
25 April 2020